"Look!" yelled Morgan above the din.

Two figures, clutching black satchels, were running toward the bus.

"Oh no!" whispered Miss Beaver faintly as one of them nearly tripped over his long skirt and threw his scarf (which had fallen over his eyes) to the ground, revealing a shaven head.

"It's the robbers!" screamed the children, jumping to their feet and chasing after Mr. Coatsworth, who was already racing after the two crooks. But they were too late. The bus engine started up, and with Sid at the wheel and Bert clinging tightly onto the door, the bus swerved out of the farmyard and careered down the drive toward the open road.

Follow That Bus!

BY PAT HUTCHINS

Illustrated by Laurence Hutchins

Bullseye Books · Alfred A. Knopf
New York

Library of Congress Catalog Card Number: 76-21822
ISBN: 0-394-80792-8
RL: 4.1

Manufactured in the United States of America
1 2 3 4 5 6 7 8 9 0

For Morgan, Dominic,
Akbar, Jessica, Avril,
and the rest of Class 6

CONTENTS

1 Raring to Go

The third grade peered anxiously out the rattling windows of the school bus as the church clock struck nine.

"There she goes!" said Mr. Coatsworth cheerfully. "At least we've got the old girl started, and now if we give her a little chance to warm up while we're waiting for Miss Beaver, she should go like a bird."

"I bet she doesn't come," said Avril mournfully.

"I bet she's been run over or something."

"Or kidnapped!" exclaimed Jessica dramatically. "I saw a program on TV once where a teacher was kidnapped. She was just walking quietly to school one day, when suddenly, out of nowhere, this big black car pulled up with a squeal of brakes . . . and then . . ."

"Perhaps she was eaten by a tiger," Akbar interrupted, knowing how long Jessica's stories took. "Tigers sometimes eat teachers in India."

"But we're not in India," said Dominic. "We're in Hampstead. And there aren't any tigers in Hampstead."

"I think she's forgotten." Morgan sighed. "Miss Beaver is always forgetting things," he added, as Jessica staggered past him, acting out the kidnapping with bloodcurdling sound effects.

"Yoo-hoo!" The familiar voice cut short Jessica's imitation of a police siren.

"Here she comes!" Morgan shouted.

"Thank goodness she's safe," said Jessica, pressing her nose to the window as Miss Beaver

raced down the hill toward them, waving a lunch-box in the air.

"Good morning, children," said Miss Beaver as she staggered onto the bus and collapsed onto the front seat. "I'm sorry I'm late, but I left my sand-wiches on the number 24 bus."

"I told you," whispered Morgan, nudging Dominic, who was sitting next to him.

"But I managed to catch up with the bus at Hampstead Hill bookshop and retrieve them," she added, holding the lunchbox up triumphantly.

"Now let me see," she continued. "I'm sure there's something I ought to do before we set off to the farm."

"Count us," said Avril.

"Of course!" exclaimed Miss Beaver. "Thank you, Avril. Now let me see, there should be twenty of you."

"Or kidnapped," Jessica interrupted. "I saw a program on TV once about some children who were kidnapped."

"Did you, dear?" Miss Beaver said hastily. "That's nice. You must tell us about it one day." She started to count rapidly.

"One, two, three . . ."

"It was like this," said Jessica, jumping down from her seat again.

"Six, seven, eight . . ." Miss Beaver paused as Jessica screamed, clutched her side, and fell flat on her face in the aisle.

"Jessica," said Miss Beaver gently, "I wonder if you would mind sitting down, dear. I keep counting you twice.

"Eighteen, nineteen, twenty," Miss Beaver finished. "Good. Now you've all remembered your raincoats and sandwiches?"

"Yes, Miss," chorused the third grade.

"In that case," said Miss Beaver, smiling at Mr. Coatsworth, "I think we can go."

"Where to, Miss?" asked Mr. Coatsworth.

"Why, to the farm of course!" said Miss Beaver brightly. "We don't want to keep Mr. and Mrs. Ramsbottom waiting. Oh dear!" she added, striking her forehead with her hand. "How silly of me! I haven't given you the address. It's written on the maps in my satchel." She started searching the floor of the bus.

"I had a copy made especially for you in case mine got mislaid, and I put both of them in the satchel. Now where did I put it?" she murmured as the children at the front of the bus got onto their hands and knees and joined in the search.

6

"Please, Miss," said Morgan, "I don't think you had a satchel."

"Oh, but I did, Morgan dear," Miss Beaver said. "I put my raincoat, my handbag, my lunchbox, and the maps in it. In fact I distinctly remember taking my lunchbox out so I could get at my purse for the bus fare."

"I didn't see you bring it on the bus either, Miss," said Avril. "Someone must have stolen it!"

"Perhaps it was a spy," said Jessica, "trying to get secret information about a deadly new substance that turns people invisible."

"Don't be silly," said Dominic. "What would a spy want with a raincoat, a handbag, and two road maps?"

"Maybe you left it on the bus," Morgan suggested.

"The bus!" Miss Beaver cried. "The bus!" she repeated. "That's where I left it. Oh dear," she said, turning to Mr. Coatsworth, "what can we do? We can't go to the farm without the maps—they have the address on them."

"Well," said Mr. Coatsworth, patting the steering wheel, "the old girl's raring to go—the number 24 bus can't have reached Camden Town yet, so let's see if we can get them back."

And as the school bus bounced forward in pursuit of the number 24 bus, two desperate robbers were holding the staff of Barclays Bank in Camden Town at gunpoint, while the terrified clerks stuffed thousands of used banknotes into their black satchels.

2 Follow That Bus!

"Look, Miss, there it is," Akbar shouted, "just in front of us, the number 24 bus."

The rest of the class crowded to the front of the bus to look. "It is, it is," cried Jessica, "and it's stopping at the bus stop!"

"Oh good!" exclaimed Miss Beaver as Mr. Coatsworth pulled in behind it.

"Shan't be a moment," she called, jumping off the school bus.

"I don't know why she's bothering," said Avril glumly. "Someone's bound to have stolen it."

"She's gone through the wrong door," said Morgan as the automatic doors opened on the number 24 bus and Miss Beaver leaped on, passing the solitary passenger who was getting off.

"Oh goodness!" Jessica squealed as the doors closed and the bus drove off again. "The driver's kidnapped our teacher!"

"Don't be silly," said Dominic as Jessica ran up and down the aisle waving her arms and shouting. "He hasn't even seen her."

"Don't worry!" said Mr. Coatsworth cheerfully. "She'll have to get off at the next stop, it's the terminal."

They could see Miss Beaver through the window—she'd found the satchel, and with a pleased smile on her face she took out one of the maps and pressed the button for the next stop.

The driver, who thought he had an empty bus, was so surprised he slammed the brakes on in an emergency stop.

"Aha!" exclaimed Mr. Coatsworth, slamming his brakes on too. The school bus screeched to a stand-still.

"Gosh!" Dominic yelled, pointing to the back of the bus. "Look!"

The rest of the class stared open-mouthed out of the back window. Heading straight toward them was a big, powerful car, and behind it, with blue lights flashing and sirens screaming, were two police cars.

"Quick!" shouted Morgan. "The floor!"

The third grade threw themselves flat on the floor. There was a tremendous crash. The bus shuddered from the impact as the big car rammed into the back of the bus, and the two police cars rammed into the back of the big car.

The children lay still for a moment, then jumped up and raced to the back windows of the bus just as two masked men, clutching black satchels and waving guns in the air, leaped out of the squashed car.

"Quick, Bert, the bus!" one of them shouted.

"Not that old clunker, you fool!" he snarled as Bert rattled the door handle of the school bus.

"That one!" He jerked his head toward the number 24 bus.

The children watched in amazement as the doors of the number 24 bus opened and Miss Beaver, who had explained all about the satchel to the driver and was stepping happily out, collided with Bert and fell backward into the bus again.

The doors closed, and before the police had even scrambled out of their wrecked cars, the bus roared off, with the driver, the two robbers, and Miss Beaver on board.

"Well!" said Mr. Coatsworth when he realized what had happened. "It takes more than a little kick up the backside to upset this old girl." He threw the bus into gear.

"What do you say, kids?"

"Follow that bus!" screamed the third grade just as the bus door opened and four disheveled policemen clambered on.

"You took the very words out of my mouth," said Sergeant Pattison grimly. Then the school bus, with a big dent in the back, leaped forward, jumped the traffic lights, and tore down the hill after the hijacked number 24 bus.

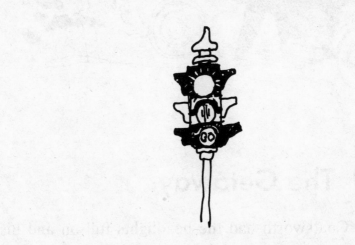

3 The Getaway

Mr. Coatsworth had the headlights full on and his hand pressed hard on the horn as he crouched over the steering wheel like a racing driver.

The children screamed for him to go faster, and

the policemen hung out of the door, shouting at cars and pedestrians to get out of the way.

But Mr. Coatsworth had his foot jammed down as far as it would go on the accelerator, and the old bus was beginning to shake with the strain.

"They're getting away!" Jessica yelled as the number 24 bus receded into the distance.

"There's too much traffic!" Morgan shouted. A car roared toward them, and Mr. Coatsworth swerved in behind a truck to avoid hitting it.

"I knew we wouldn't get to the farm," Avril complained. "I've never been to a farm before," she added bitterly as the number 24 vanished over the rim of a hill.

"Oh no!" groaned the children, for not only had the bus disappeared, but holding up the traffic at the crossroads was an enormous trailer truck.

Mr. Coatsworth ground the school bus to a halt and mopped his face while the children hopped up and down impatiently.

The policemen waved wildly for the truck to move on, but the driver just shrugged and pointed to the line of cars in front of him.

"We'll never catch up with them now," Dominic sighed as the truck inched its way slowly across their path.

"Poor Miss Beaver," Jessica said, "she was my most favorite teacher *ever*!"

By the time the path was clear and the bus had roared off again, half the smaller children in the class had burst into tears at Jessica's vivid description of the dreadful things she thought would happen to their teacher in the hands of two desperate robbers.

They followed the road that the number 24 bus had taken, but could see no sign of it.

"It's no good," said Mr. Coatsworth as they dropped over the hill where they'd last seen it. "We might as well stop; they must be miles away by now."

"Wait a minute!" said Morgan excitedly, running up to the front window. "I think I can see something."

"I can't," said Sergeant Pattison, squinting into the distance.

"Neither can we," said the other policemen.

"I'm sure I can," said Morgan, who had eyes like a hawk. "Look! Pulled off the road ahead."

The rest of the class ran to the front of the bus to look, but they couldn't see anything either.

"By George!" said Sergeant Pattison, grabbing Mr. Coatsworth's arm and making the bus swerve. "I believe the boy's right. Well done, lad!" he shouted. A small red dot appeared in the distance and gradually got bigger as the bus advanced toward it.

"It's the bus! It's the bus!" screamed the children.

"Why has it stopped?" asked Dominic.

"We'll soon find out," said Mr. Coatsworth grimly, coaxing the bus to go even faster.

"There's Miss Beaver!" Morgan cried as they got nearer the number 24 bus. "She's safe!"

"And the driver too!" shouted Akbar.

They shivered to a stop behind the number 24 bus.

The children scrambled off the bus, tripping up the policemen, who were trying to get off as well.

"Are you all right, Miss?" asked Sergeant Pattison, picking himself up and dusting his uniform down.

"Oh perfectly!" exclaimed Miss Beaver, her face pink with excitement as the children surrounded her, all talking at once.

"And you, sir?" he asked the driver, who was sitting on the grass looking slightly dazed. The driver nodded gloomily. "We ran out of gas," he muttered. "They went that way," he added, pointing across the fields, "and they took the money with them."

"Right!" said Sergeant Pattison briskly. "Smith and Pike, you come with me. Turner, I want you to find a telephone and call for help." Then he leaped over the fence and disappeared across the fields.

And while Miss Beaver made a statement for the police, Mr. Coatsworth raised the hood of the bus to let the engine cool down and poured some hot, sweet tea out of his thermos for the driver, who was still looking a bit stunned by it all.

"Well, children," said Miss Beaver, after she'd

answered all the policeman's questions and the driver
had been taken back to the bus terminal in one of
the police cars that had arrived.

"I've got my satchel back"—she patted the black
satchel in her hand—"and we have the map." She
waved the map she'd been clutching in the air. "So
let's go to the farm."

"About time, too," Avril muttered.

"Oh!" moaned the rest of the class, who were all
for following the sergeant across the fields.

"What a coincidence!" exclaimed Mr. Coatsworth, taking the piece of paper and looking at it. "We've been following the route to the farm all along. It's only a mile or so from here," he added, snapping the hood of the bus shut. "We'll be there in no time!"

"I wish we'd found the robbers," Morgan whispered to Dominic as they climbed onto the bus again.

"I don't," announced Miss Beaver, who had overheard him. "I think we've had quite enough excitement for one day," she finished, closing the bus door.

4 Meadow Farm

"We must be quite near the farm now," said Miss Beaver, looking at the map as the bus bumped over a railroad crossing. "It's very close to the station.

"Just think, children," she added, although none

of the children, except Avril, seemed terribly interested in visiting the farm now. They were talking excitedly about the robbery and the bus chase. "Just think!" she repeated, raising her voice above the chatter. "We might see some cows being milked if we're lucky."

"Or a bull," said Avril. "I've never seen a bull before."

"They don't milk bulls," said Dominic flatly, thinking, like the rest of the class, how he'd much rather be chasing robbers across the fields than watching cows being milked.

"I know that!" said Avril scornfully. "I know all about bulls. My dad told me how they could toss a man in the air, catch him on their horns, then trample him to death."

"Oooh!" whispered Jessica, suddenly becoming interested in visiting the farm again. "How *awful*! I read a story once about a great big bull, with absolutely *enormous* horns, and one day . . ."

"Left here, Mr. Coatsworth," Miss Beaver interrupted hastily as the bus reached a crossroads.

"I don't suppose they'll have a bull anyway." Avril sighed.

Mr. Coatsworth swung the bus into a narrow lane, making Jessica, who had spotted an open-mouthed audience of younger children at the back of the bus and was on her way to finish the story, stumble and fall onto her hands and knees.

"Are you all right, Jessica dear?" Miss Beaver asked anxiously.

"Of course, Miss," said Jessica stiffly, still eye-ing her audience from the floor. Then, holding her hands up to her head like horns, she bellowed loudly to the wide-eyed children before standing up, dust-ing herself down, and walking with great dignity back to her seat.

"I was just being a bull," she said, "that's all."

Miss Beaver waited until Jessica was safely seated before studying her map again.

"According to the map," she said, "we should be almost there."

"There it is, Miss," said Morgan, pointing into the distance where he could see a sign with MEADOW FARM written on it.

"I wish we didn't have to go," he added wistfully. "I wish we could have gone with the sergeant instead."

"So do we, Miss," shouted the rest of the third grade (except for Avril, who had her nose pressed to the window, scanning the countryside anxiously for any sign of a ferocious bull).

"Well, you never know!" Mr. Coatsworth laughed as the bus turned into the driveway of the farm. "They might even be lurking around here someplace."

"Oh dear!" said Miss Beaver in alarm. "I hope not! Anyway," she added nervously, "I'm sure the police will have caught them by now."

"Just joking, Miss," said Mr. Coatsworth, stopping the bus in front of the farmhouse.

"Although I must admit," he added, chuckling and slapping the steering wheel, "I've not enjoyed myself so much for ages."

"We'll keep our eyes open," Morgan hissed in his ear as Miss Beaver opened the door, "just in case."

"Is this it?" demanded Avril when all the children were off the bus. She paused to look at the ramshackle barn, the chicken coop, and the pigpen with three sleepy pigs in it. "It's very small," she said darkly, "and I can't see any bull."

"I can see two, I can see two!" screamed Jessica, tugging at the teacher's arm and pointing to a field.

"They're cows," said Dominic. One of them bent its head, blinked its velvety eyes, and lowed gently at them.

"Are you sure?" whispered Jessica, grabbing hold of Miss Beaver's hand. "They look like bulls to me!"

"Ah well," Morgan murmured as Jessica darted among the children, arguing about the difference between cows and bulls. "At least they've got a tractor and trailer," Morgan said. He brightened up

a bit as he nudged Dominic. "They might give us a ride on it if we ask."

"Now then, children, calm down," said Miss Beaver briskly. Jessica had somehow managed (without going herself) to coax a group of confused and nervous children to approach the fence and study the two animals to prove they were really and truly cows.

"You've all got your raincoats and sandwiches, haven't you?" Miss Beaver looked at her watch.

"After we've introduced ourselves to Mr. and Mrs."—she fumbled in her pocket for the map—"Ramsbottom," she read. "We'll look around the farm, then have a little picnic in the field."

The smaller children looked uncertainly at the cows.

"That field," said Miss Beaver, pointing to the next field, which didn't have any animals in it, as she wasn't too sure about cows either.

"I'll tinker about with the old bus while you're looking around," said Mr. Coatsworth. "She had a bit of a rough ride this morning, poor old girl."

"Here, Miss," he added, handing Miss Beaver

her satchel. "Don't for-
get your bag. You know
what happened last time
you left it on a bus," he
said laughingly.

"Can I carry your bag,
Miss?" asked Avril. "As
there isn't a bull?"

"Of course, Avril
dear," said Miss Beaver,
handing the satchel to
Avril.

"Look, Miss," said Akbar as the farmhouse
door creaked open, "there's the farmer and his
wife."

"Come on, children," said Miss Beaver gaily.
"Let's go and meet them."

And as she marched up to the farmhouse, with
the children straggling halfheartedly behind, Miss
Beaver had to admit to herself that never, in all her
life, had she seen anyone as remarkably ugly as the
farmer.

Excepting, perhaps, his unfortunate wife.

5 Mr. and Mrs. Ramsbottom

The children stared at the couple in amazement.

They could hardly believe their eyes.

The farmer was ugly enough, with his tiny, close-set eyes and his squashed nose, and the hideous scars that ran across his face from one cauliflower ear to the other.

But his wife! She was incredible!!! She was dressed in what looked like a long nightdress and rubber boots. The scarf she had wrapped around her huge head and tied under her enormous chin managed to conceal some of the face. But the bit that showed was astonishing.

Her face was so thick with powder she looked as if someone had tipped a bag of flour over her head and she'd forgotten to blow afterward. Her stubby eyelashes were white, her thick bushy eyebrows were white, and even the rims of her watery eyes were white. And somehow near the bottom of the whiteness was a gash of brilliant red lipstick, which covered the whole of her mouth and most of her chin. She had a broken nose, and when she smiled coyly at them, her front two teeth were missing.

"Gosh!" whispered Avril, instinctively taking a step backward with the rest of the class.

"Hello," said Miss Beaver bravely, holding her hand out hesitantly to the farmer. "You must be"—she fumbled for the map again and looked at it—"Mr. Ramsbottom."

"Yeah," said the farmer, nudging his wife, "Ramsbottom. That's our name."

"And you must be Mrs. Ramsbottom," Miss Beaver added, offering her hand to the farmer's wife, as the farmer had ignored it.

The farmer's wife grunted and shuffled her feet.

"She don't say much," the farmer said, tapping his forehead and nudging his wife again. "On account of she's got a few screws loose."

"Oh!" said Miss Beaver, startled by the farmer's bluntness. "I'm Miss Beaver from New End School," she added nervously, "and this is the third grade."

"Whaddaya say!" the farmer said, glancing furtively at the children. His eyes rested on Avril, who was clutching the teacher's satchel tightly, mesmerized by the farmer's wife.

" 'Ere," he said, taking a step toward her. "What's a little tiddler like you doing heaving a great heavy bag like that around for?"

He bent down and looked into Avril's eyes.

"I'll carry it for you," he said coaxingly.

Avril gripped the handle even tighter.

"You don't have a bull," she said accusingly.

"What?" said the farmer, stepping back in surprise. Miss Beaver laughed uncertainly.

"I'm afraid Avril was rather disappointed that you didn't have a bull," she explained, "so I said she could carry my bag. It isn't heavy," she added. "It only has my handbag and raincoat in it."

"Well, I wouldn't want you to think I wasn't no gentleman, now, would I?" said the farmer, gritting his yellow teeth into a grin and tugging at the bottom of the satchel.

Avril put both arms around the bag and pulled back, staring defiantly at the farmer, whose grin was fading rapidly.

"I expect she'll get tired of carrying it soon," Miss Beaver said hastily, not wanting to hurt the farmer's feelings.

The farmer muttered to himself and let go suddenly. "Yeah!" he said, scowling, as Avril fell backward. "She'd better—I mean I'd feel better," he added quickly, helping an indignant Avril to her feet, "carrying it myself."

He lowered his voice and clasped his hands together tightly. "You see, I just love children. And it breaks my heart to think of the poor little things going and straining themselves, like. You know what I mean?"

Miss Beaver nodded politely, although she didn't know what he meant at all.

The children had begun whispering amongst themselves, and Miss Beaver, not wanting the farmer and his wife to overhear them, said very loudly, "It was awfully kind of you to offer to show us around the farm, but I'm sure we can manage on our own, can't we, children?" She turned desperately to the children, who were whispering even louder now, and she was sure she heard Jessica murmur "Frankenstein" in Akbar's ear.

"YOU MUST BE TERRIBLY BUSY!" she

shouted at the farmer, trying to drown out the children's conversation.

"No, we ain't," said the farmer. "We ain't got nothing to do but show you around, have we, Missus?" He dug his elbow into his wife, who didn't seem to hear him as she stared foolishly at the ground.

"HAVE WE, MISSUS?" he repeated, clipping his wife smartly around the ear.

"Hey. Watch it!" his wife replied in a gruff, reproachful voice.

"Just a little playful kidding around," said the farmer, laughing as he raised his fist and thumped his wife violently between the shoulder blades.

"The poor old girl's got a touch of laryngitis, ain't yer?" he roared in her ear.

His wife nodded slowly, then, lifting her muscular arm, sent the farmer flying with a return clout.

The farmer staggered to his feet and advanced menacingly toward his wife.

The children held their breath, waiting for the blow

to fall. But the farmer, instead of hitting her, tweaked his wife playfully on the cheek.

"As I was saying," he said cheerfully to Miss Beaver, who was beginning to look a bit alarmed, "just a little playful kidding around. Now," he added, glancing slyly at the breathless children and nudging his wife yet again, "to show these little darlings around."

Dominic prodded Morgan, who had edged his way to the front of the class.

"Please, sir," said Morgan politely, "you haven't seen two masked men around, have you? There was a robbery and we chased them, but they got away."

"Masked men?" the farmer repeated vaguely. "We ain't seen no masked men, have we, Missus?" He thrust his face close to his wife's.

His wife shook her head vigorously.

"We ain't seen nothing," she squeaked in a falsetto voice.

Goodness, thought Miss Beaver, her laryngitis has cleared up quickly.

"Oh!" said Morgan, disappointed.

Dominic nudged Morgan again.

"Then please could we have a ride on your tractor?" he added quickly.

"Please, Miss, I'm starving to death," Jessica complained. "Can't we have our picnic first?"

"I don't want to ride on any tractor," Avril said. "I want to look around the farm."

"We want a ride on the tractor too, Miss," the rest of the third grade chorused.

"Well," said the farmer, stroking his chin thoughtfully. "I think I can keep you all happy, you know what I mean? The missus here can show Avril around the farm"—he patted Avril gently on the cheek, and winked slowly at his wife—"while I give the rest of you kids a quick turn on the tractor before you has your nosh."

Avril looked at the wife doubtfully, but finally muttered, "All right." The rest of the class, led by Miss Beaver, followed the farmer across to the tractor and trailer.

As Avril, still clutching the satchel tightly, went into the barn with the farmer's wife, she noticed, with surprise, a faint stubble of whiskers protruding through the thick white powder on Mrs. Ramsbottom's face.

41

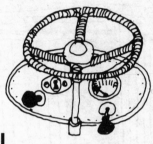

6 The Robbers!

The children waited impatiently while the farmer, glancing furtively over his shoulder toward the barn all the time, fiddled with the knobs on the tractor.

"I don't think he knows how to drive it," Morgan whispered to Dominic. The farmer pressed every button and tapped every dial on the dashboard, but still couldn't get the engine started.

"Please, sir," said one of the little children, who was still not sure about the cows in the field. "Are they cows or bulls over there?"

"Is what cows or bulls?" asked the farmer, looking around vaguely.

"There!" said Jessica, stabbing her finger at the field. The farmer looked confused for a moment, then catching Dominic's eye, said, "You look like a smart lad, tell her what they are."

"Cows!" said Dominic proudly.

"Yeah!" said the farmer. "Cows. That's what they are."

"And what breed are the pigs?" Miss Beaver asked politely, as the farmer started kicking the tractor angrily, still peering anxiously in the direction of the barn.

"Pigs," said the farmer, "what pigs?"

"Why those," said Miss Beaver, glancing at the three sleepy pigs. The farmer looked at the pigs in desperation.

"Let's see," he said, stroking his chin. "Any smart kid know what breed these pigs is?"

The third grade shook their heads.

The farmer looked relieved. "They're longhorns, ain't they?" he said.

"Please, sir," said Jessica, "I thought longhorns were cattle. I saw a film once, where a cowboy was trampled to death by longhorns . . ."

"Aha," interrupted the farmer, scowling at Jessica, "just trying to catch you out. You know what I mean?

"They're shorthorns," he added fiercely, thrusting his face toward Jessica's.

Jessica stepped back nervously, then the farmer's scowl changed to an oily smile.

"Sharp as a razor blade, this 'un," he said to Miss Beaver, patting Jessica gently on her cheek.

The children were beginning to feel very hungry as they stood watching the farmer kicking the tractor and jerking his head toward the barn between each kick. They were quite relieved when Mr. Coatsworth stuck his head out of the bus and shouted, "You forgot your lunch, Miss," and jumped down from the bus to join them, carrying Miss Beaver's sandwiches and his own packed lunch.

"Please, Miss," said Jessica, clutching her stomach. "I'm absolutely dying of starvation. I can't go another minute," she added dramatically, "without food."

"Neither can we, Miss," said the rest of the class, realizing that the chances of a ride on the tractor were getting very slim.

"Here!" Mr. Coatsworth laughed and pulled a large bag of candy from his pocket. "Have a licorice ball to keep you going."

The children lost interest in the farmer when they saw the bag, and crowded around Mr. Coatsworth as he handed out the candy.

The farmer had lost interest in the children too, and was staring openly at the barn.

"I think," said Miss Beaver, "that if you don't mind we'd better have our picnic now." She glanced at her watch. "It's getting rather close to lunchtime."

"Yeah!" muttered the farmer, shading his eyes and staring past her. "The old geezer don't seem to want to go anyway." His eyes suddenly lit up as he caught a glimpse of his wife, lurking by the side of the house and beckoning furiously to him.

"I'm feeling a bit hungry myself," he said slowly. "I think I'll go and get some grub too."

Mr. Coatsworth offered him a licorice ball. "Thanks!" he said, grabbing a huge handful and stuffing them in his pocket. Then, strolling casually toward the farmhouse, he threw one high in the air and caught it in his gaping mouth.

What a strange gentleman, Miss Beaver thought as she and Mr. Coatsworth followed the children to the empty field.

"Here's a good spot, Miss," Akbar said, spreading his raincoat on the damp grass and sitting down.

Miss Beaver watched the rest of the children spreading their raincoats out too, thinking she would do the same, when she realized that hers was in the bag that Avril was carrying. She looked around, but couldn't see any sign of Avril.

"Has anyone seen Avril?" she asked.

"She went off with the farmer's wife," said Akbar, "to look around the farm."

"That's funny," said Morgan. "I saw the farmer's wife go into the house, but Avril wasn't with her."

"Oh dear," said Miss Beaver. "I do hope she hasn't got lost. I think perhaps we ought to go and look for her," she added nervously.

"There she is!" Dominic shouted as a disheveled figure came tearing toward them, shouting at the top of its voice.

"Good heavens!" exclaimed Miss Beaver, grabbing Mr. Coatsworth's arm. "Whatever is happening?"

For not only was Avril shouting, but the bedroom window of the farmhouse had suddenly been thrown open, and two complete strangers, waving their arms wildly in the air, joined in the shouting too.

And in the distance, yelping dogs, whinnying horses, and huntsmen's horns added to the commotion.

"Look!" yelled Morgan above the din.

Two figures, clutching black satchels, were running toward the bus.

"Oh no!" whispered Miss Beaver faintly as one of them nearly tripped over his long skirt and threw the scarf (which had fallen over his eyes) to the ground, revealing a shaved head.

"It's the robbers!" screamed the children, jumping to their feet and chasing after Mr. Coatsworth, who was already racing after the two crooks.

But they were too late. The bus engine started up, and with Sid at the wheel and Bert clinging tightly onto the door, the bus swerved out of the farmyard and careered down the drive toward the open road.

"Quick, kids! Into the trailer!" shouted Mr. Coatsworth, jumping into the driving seat of the tractor. Avril and Miss Beaver caught up with the rest of the class and threw themselves into the trailer too.

And as the tractor's engine roared to life, they didn't even notice Sergeant Pattison and his men staggering wearily into the farmyard with a pack of snapping foxhounds at their heels, and the confused members of the County Hunt galloping behind them.

7 The Tractor Chase

The children were wild with excitement. They bounced and swayed in the trailer, shouting and screaming at Mr. Coatsworth, urging him to go faster as he desperately tried to catch up with the retreating bus.

"He locked me in the barn," Avril kept yelling indignantly. "When I said I thought he was really a guy, he grabbed the bag and locked me in the barn."

"But what on earth did he want with my bag?" Miss Beaver interrupted.

"And why were they pretending to be Mr. and Mrs. Ramsbottom?" asked Akbar.

"And how did they know we were going to the farm?" Dominic demanded.

"I still think they're spies," said Jessica wildly, "trying to get secret information about a deadly new substance that turns people invisible."

Dominic sighed. "I told you before," he said. "A raincoat, a handbag, and a road map aren't any use to a spy. Anyway," he added, "they're robbers, not spies."

Morgan, who had been listening to the conversation with a funny look on his face, jumped up suddenly.

"That's it!" he shouted.

The children stopped screaming at Mr. Coatsworth and looked at Morgan in astonishment.

"That's it!" he repeated, hanging on to the side of the trailer to steady himself. "The map!"

"See!" said Jessica proudly. "Morgan thinks they were after Miss Beaver's bag too!"

"But they didn't want Miss Beaver's bag!" Morgan cried. "Don't you see?" He turned to Miss Beaver. "Your satchel is exactly the same as the two they had. They must have got mixed up when they hijacked the number 24 bus, and when they discovered the map in your bag, they knew we were going to the farm."

"So they disguised themselves as Mr. and Mrs. Ramsbottom," Dominic added slowly, "to try and get their satchel back!"

"Then that strange couple at the window must be the real farmer and his wife!" gasped Miss Beaver.

"And I," shrieked Avril, "have been walking around all morning with half their loot!"

"Well," Mr. Coatsworth shouted over his shoulder, "they've got it all now. And it looks like they'll get away with it too," he added, as the bus pulled even farther away from them and headed toward the level crossing.

"Look!" shouted Morgan, who had spotted a train in the distance and the stationmaster hurrying toward the gate to close it. "They'll have to stop!"

But the robbers didn't stop. And the stationmas-

ter, who had already started to close the gate, pulled it back in amazement as the bus roared through the gap, bounced safely over the track, and landed on the other side of the road.

"If they can do it," Mr. Coatsworth yelled, jamming his foot hard on the accelerator, "so can we!"

The stationmaster, who had started closing the gate again, saw the tractor and trailer heading toward

him at full tilt and, leaping onto the gate, swung
back with his eyes tightly closed.

"Please, Miss," Akbar shouted as the express
thundered toward them, "I can hear dogs barking!"

But Miss Beaver and the rest of the children (who
had their eyes tightly closed too) didn't hear him.
The huge engine, missing them by inches, tore down
the line behind them.

"Or I thought I could," Akbar murmured to himself, glancing back at the engine and the long line of swaying coaches that rattled along the track.

The children opened their eyes again as the tractor and trailer turned a bend in the road.

Mr. Coatsworth braked suddenly, throwing the children on top of one another.

"Good heavens!" exclaimed Miss Beaver. "It's stopped!"

Mr. Coatsworth jumped down from the tractor and looked suspiciously at the bus in the distance. It was parked at such an angle that, although they could see the rear of it, the door and driving cab were completely hidden by the curve in the road.

"We'd better be careful," he murmured. "It might be a trap. I think you kids had better stay here while we investigate." He nodded to Miss Beaver, who nodded back weakly, wishing Mr. Coatsworth had said "I" instead of "we."

"Remember, they have a gun," Miss Beaver said nervously as the children complained.

"And if we get the bus back—I mean when—" she added quickly, "we're going straight back to the farm to have our lunch, robbers or no robbers."

"Please, Miss," said Jessica miserably, "they may as well shoot me, I'm half dead from hunger already."

"Here," said Mr. Coatsworth, pulling the half-empty bag of candy from his pocket. "Share them out while you're waiting."

And while the children sucked slowly on their licorice balls, Miss Beaver and Mr. Coatsworth crept cautiously up the road toward the school bus, completely unaware of the village policeman cycling furiously toward it from the opposite direction.

8 A Dreadful Mistake

"They're not in the bus," whispered Mr. Coatsworth. He and Miss Beaver stood on tiptoe and pressed their noses against the bus window. "They must have made off across the fields."

"Look!" cried Miss Beaver, pointing to the corridor. "They've dropped something."

They clambered onto the bus to see what it was. Mr. Coatsworth whistled as he bent down and picked the object up.

"They certainly did drop something," he said grimly, handing it carefully to Miss Beaver, who gazed at it in horror.

"Aha!" said a voice behind them.

Miss Beaver spun around in alarm, the gun falling from her hand.

"Oh!" she cried in relief, seeing the policeman dive to the floor to pick it up. "Thank goodness!"

"So," said the policeman, clutching the gun nervously. "Saw me coming, eh? Frightened, eh?? Thought you'd do a little disappearing act, eh???"

"No!" said Miss Beaver in surprise.

"Oh!" said the policeman, shifting his feet awkwardly and looking a bit put out.

"Ready to cooperate then?" he added hopefully.

"Of course!" said Miss Beaver, smiling.

"And you, sir?" The policeman looked warily at Mr. Coatsworth.

"Certainly," said Mr. Coatsworth.

"Good!" said the policeman. "Hold out your hands."

Mr. Coatsworth and Miss Beaver looked at each other in surprise, shrugged, and held their hands out.

"Hey!" shouted Mr. Coatsworth as the policeman snapped a pair of handcuffs onto one of his wrists.

"Goodness!" said Miss Beaver, looking down at her wrist, which was now firmly attached to Mr. Coatsworth.

"Ha!" said the policeman, wagging his finger at the astonished Miss Beaver. "A good disguise. A very good disguise. Could fool a lot of people. But not me," he finished proudly. "Now. Where's the money?"

Miss Beaver looked at Mr. Coatsworth in alarm.

"What on earth is the man talking about?" she asked.

Mr. Coatsworth, who had been looking just as bewildered as Miss Beaver, suddenly slapped his leg with his free hand and burst out laughing. The policeman gripped the gun tightly in his hand and looked at him uneasily.

"So," he said. "Think we won't find it, eh? Hidden it under a seat, eh??" He waved the gun wildly around the bus. "Or maybe in the luggage rack, eh???"

Mr. Coatsworth shook with laughter, tears rolling down his face.

"I'm sorry," he gasped, looking at Miss Beaver's anxious face. He slapped his leg again to try and stifle his laughter.

"He thinks we're the robbers," he spluttered, "and that you're really a man!"

"Oh!" said Miss Beaver, not sure whether to laugh or not.

The policeman's eyes narrowed suspiciously. "Now look here," he said uncomfortably. "You won't catch me out with any of your little games. I know exactly who you are. Sergeant Pattison telephoned me from the farm. Two fellows"—he jerked the gun at Mr. Coatsworth and then Miss Beaver—"one dressed as a woman," he added darkly, "driving a bus." He waved the gun around the bus again.

"And armed with a gun," he finished, glancing down at the gun.

Miss Beaver laughed awkwardly. "But you've made a dreadful mistake," she protested. "I am Miss Beaver from New End School, and this is Mr. Coatsworth, the school driver."

"Oh yes!" said the policeman sarcastically. "And I'm Napoleon."

"Well, Constable Napoleon," said Miss Beaver, shaking her wrist, "perhaps you'll take these silly things off now. My children are very hungry and it's past their lunchtime."

"Yes," said the policeman slowly, eyeing the empty bus.

"They look hungry, very hungry. In fact so hungry that they've faded away," he added, laughing dryly at his own joke.

"The children," Miss Beaver said coldly, "are not in the bus."

Mr. Coatsworth wiped his eyes with the back of his free hand. "They're down the road a bit," he said, trying not to laugh, "in a trailer."

"Down the road a bit, eh?" the policeman repeated. "In a trailer, eh?? That's a good one!"

"Go and see for yourself if you don't believe us," said Miss Beaver crossly.

"Ha!" said the policeman. "You'd like that, eh? Get me off the bus, eh?? Drive off and leave me behind, eh???"

"Oh dear!" said Miss Beaver wearily. "Then we'll come with you if you like."

"That's better," said the policeman, and with the gun still pointed at them, he backed out of the bus, lifted his bicycle into it, and closed the door behind him.

"And you'd better come quietly, mind," he added. "I've got the gun now, remember."

"Good heavens!" said Miss Beaver weakly. "The man's gone mad."

And to Miss Beaver's and Mr. Coatsworth's astonishment, the policeman, who had never driven a car before in his life, let alone a bus, climbed into the driver's seat.

9 A Dirty Double Cross

The children were beginning to get tired of waiting and climbed out of the trailer to stretch their legs.

"Do you think they've been shot?" Jessica whispered, popping another licorice ball into her mouth. "And that they're too weak to call for help?"

"No," murmured Morgan, who was shading his eyes with his hand and squinting across the fields.

"We would have heard the explosion," Dominic added, gazing at the back of the bus, trying in vain to see what was going on inside it.

"I bet the robbers have got them though," said Avril bitterly. "I bet they've tied them up and

dumped them in the hedge and we'll never get back
to the farm."

"What about our lunch?" wailed the children.
"We're starving."

"Perhaps we'll all starve to death," said Jessica
solemnly, "and our bones won't be found for years,
and years, and years . . ."

"Listen!" Akbar interrupted. "I can hear those
dogs again."

"You don't think they're wolves, do you?" cried Jessica, grabbing his arm in alarm.

"I saw a program on TV once about a group of children who were slowly starving to death at the North Pole, and the wolves waited and waited until they were too weak to fight, and then . . ."

"Look!" screamed Avril, pointing to the bus. "The bus! It's moving!"

"Oooh!" squealed Jessica. "It's the robbers! They've kidnapped our teacher again!"

"Wait!" Morgan shouted as the children started running after the bus. He waved his arms frantically in the direction of the field. "It can't be the robbers! There they are!"

The children turned to see two small figures disappearing over the top of a hill.

"Quick, after them!" yelled Morgan, climbing over the fence. The rest of the children ran back in confusion.

"Oh no!" gasped Akbar, glancing over his shoulder as he stumbled through the long grass after

Morgan. "We're being followed by a pack of hounds!"

Dominic looked over his shoulder too, and shook his head in disbelief.

For galloping wildly down the road after the school bus, clinging tightly to each other and the neck of the horse they had commandeered (and were sharing between them), were Sergeant Pattison and his men, hotly pursued by the members of the County Hunt in full cry, and Mr. and Mrs. Ramsbottom on an ancient tandem bicycle. But the dogs, instead of staying with the hunters, had sniffed the trailer, jumped the fence, and, ignoring the huntsmen's angry cries, run yapping and whining across the fields after the children.

"Help!" shrieked Jessica as one of the hounds caught up with her, knocked her over, and started licking her face furiously. "I'm being eaten alive!"

"So am I!" gasped Avril as a bunch of dogs ran between her legs, tripped her up, and started licking her too.

"And me!"

"And me!" The shout echoed across the fields as one by one the children were knocked off their feet and their faces licked clean by the excited hounds.

Morgan, who was well ahead of them and didn't hear the commotion, stopped suddenly in his tracks. For just in front of him, clutching a black satchel and desperately trying to free his long nightdress from a thorn bush, was Bert.

Morgan closed his eyes, took a deep breath, then lunged at Bert's feet, hanging on for grim death and shouting at the top of his voice, until the rest of the children, realizing that the dogs weren't going to eat them after all, scrambled to their feet and stumbled up the hill after him.

"Help, Sid, help!" Bert screamed, furiously shaking his foot to try and free it when he saw the third grade and the pack of hounds heading toward him. But Sid, instead of going to his crony's aid, leaped over a hedge and ran off as fast as his legs would carry him, laughing maliciously.

Before Bert had time to open his mouth again, the third grade leaped at him. His long nightdress tore free and he was pinned to the ground.

The hounds, beside themselves with excitement, leaped on him too, but after sniffing the bit of him that wasn't smothered by children, lost interest, and poked their wet noses into the children's pockets instead.

Morgan looked across the fields to where Sid had disappeared and frowned.

"It's a pity he got away," he murmured. "Still," he added, picking up the satchel that Bert had dropped, "at least we've got half the money."

"What are we going to do now?" Dominic asked as the children bounced up and down on Bert's stomach. "We can't sit on him forever!"

"Torture him," said Avril grimly, twisting one of his ears. "That's for locking me in the barn," she muttered ferociously, "and that"—she twisted his other ear—"is for taking the bag."

"Shout," said Morgan. "Someone's bound to hear us."

"I wonder what happened to Miss Beaver and Mr. Coatsworth," Akbar said as the children shouted at the top of their lungs.

"There they are!" Jessica shrieked. "Look!"

Hurrying across the fields toward them were Miss Beaver and Mr. Coatsworth, and limping behind them were Sergeant Pattison and his men (who had been thrown off the horse so many times, they'd decided it was safer to walk), and shuffling behind them was the red-faced village policeman, and behind the village policeman were the farmer and his wife, and galloping up in the rear were the indignant members of the County Hunt.

"Look, everyone!" Avril shouted, snatching the satchel from Morgan and waving it in the air.

Bert lifted his head wearily to have one last look at his loot.

"Oh no!" cried the children in horror, for as Avril swung the bag, the catch broke and the satchel dropped open.

"The dirty double-crosser!" Bert snarled. A raincoat, a handbag, and a road map fell out.

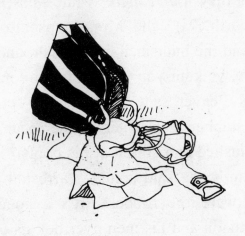

10 Licorice Balls!

The children stared at the satchel silently, too disappointed even to bother to push away the hounds that were ferreting in their pockets and eating any licorice balls they found there, while Miss Beaver, Mr. Coatsworth, Mr. and Mrs. Ramsbottom, the policemen, and the huntsmen crowded around them.

"I'm sorry we kept you waiting for so long, children," Miss Beaver said breathlessly, "but that, that"—she stabbed her finger at the local policeman, who blushed and stared at his boots.

"Policeman," she said coldly, "arrested us. He thought *we* were the robbers. It's a good thing Sergeant Pattison and his men overtook us on their

horse and flagged him down, or goodness knows what would have happened to us. He was driving the bus like a maniac . . .

"Oh my goodness!" she gasped when she caught a glimpse of Bert's desperate face from under the pile of bodies. "It's that woman—I mean man! Oh dear," she added in concern, "are you all right, children?"

The children nodded halfheartedly.

"They might be all right," gasped Bert, "but I ain't. They're knocking the stuffing out of me."

"Serves you right!" snapped Mrs. Ramsbottom, who was circling him looking for a bit of flesh to get at, until Avril obligingly stood up, revealing a hairy arm where the nightdress had torn.

"I've a good mind to set Mr. Ramsbottom onto you," she added, pinching his arm fiercely with her plump fingers and jerking her head toward her timid husband, who was grinning weakly and backing away from them.

"There, there," said Sergeant Pattison soothingly as Mrs. Ramsbottom raised her handbag above Bert's head. "He'll get what's coming to him."

She lowered her handbag reluctantly.

"What about that other fellow?" she demanded.

"He went that way," said Morgan miserably, pointing across the fields, "but we'll never catch him now, and he's got all the money."

"Never mind, lad," said Sergeant Pattison kindly, "at least you've caught one of them, and we'll get the other one eventually, don't you worry."

"And you did get my satchel back," Miss Beaver added, trying to cheer them up a bit.

"What I want to know," interrupted the leader of the hunt crossly, "is what you children have done to our hounds. They've been going berserk since they got your scent!"

"Huh!" Avril snorted, trying unsuccessfully to push away a dog that was licking her. "It's not what we've been doing to your hounds. It's what your hounds have been doing to us!"

"They've been trying to eat us," Jessica added

indignantly, "just like that program on TV where the wolves knew the children were starving to death and were too weak and hungry to fight back."

"Ha-ha!" muttered Bert mirthlessly, rubbing his smarting ears.

"Hey!" Akbar shouted as a dog poked its nose into his pocket. "It's taken my last licorice ball!"

"And mine!" said Dominic.

"And mine!" the rest of the class shouted, feeling in their pockets.

"LICORICE BALLS!" the leader of the hunt thundered. "You haven't been feeding them LICORICE BALLS!!"

"We didn't feed them any licorice balls," said Avril flatly. "They stole them."

"Licorice balls," the huntsman repeated, turning to the other riders, who threw their hands up in horror. "Would you believe it?

"Don't you realize," he added fiercely, staring at Avril, "that hounds will follow the trail of licorice *anywhere*?! No wonder they've been acting peculiar."

"Well, they've eaten them all now," said Avril, eyeing the dogs with a murderous look as they sat happily munching the last of the candy.

"And we're starving," said Jessica accusingly.

"Well," said Miss Beaver decisively, "we're going back to the farm to finish our picnic now, if Mr. and Mrs.—er . . ." she paused to pull the map out of her pocket, "Ramsbottom," she read, "don't mind."

The farmer grinned, quite relieved to have an excuse to get away. "Not at all," he said. "I'm feeling a bit hungry myself."

"How strange," Miss Beaver murmured, frowning thoughtfully to herself, "that's exactly what that dreadful man said the last time I suggested lunch; and Mr. Coatsworth here offered him a licorice ball.''

"And the rogue took a handful," added Mr. Coatsworth, shaking his head at the thought.

"AND STUFFED THEM IN HIS POCKET!" Morgan shouted, jumping up and staring at the hounds, who seemed to have lost interest in the children now that all the candy was gone and were sniffing in the direction of the fields.

"And they said," Sergeant Pattison murmured, glancing at the huntsman, "that . . ."

"A HOUND WILL FOLLOW THE TRAIL OF LICORICE ANYWHERE!" screamed the children.

And before Miss Beaver had time to protest, the children were on their feet and tearing after the hounds, who had caught the scent of more licorice and were yapping and barking excitedly as they bounded across the fields.

"Come on, men!" yelled Sergeant Pattison. "Follow those hounds!" and leaving the bewil-

dered village policeman to take care of Bert, he and his men chased after them, followed by Miss Beaver, Mr. Coatsworth, and Mrs. Ramsbottom, dragging her reluctant husband behind her.

"Yoicks! Tallyho!" shouted the leader of the hunt, not wanting to miss out on a chase, and with a blast on the horn, the County Hunt charged forward too.

11 Captured

The children raced after the baying hounds, their legs aching and their hearts pounding.

"We're heading back toward the farm," Akbar gasped, recognizing the farmyard in the distance.

"I can see our sandwiches," said Jessica longingly.

"I bet we won't catch him," Avril grumbled. "I bet he's got away."

"No, he hasn't," Morgan yelled, spotting a tiny figure just in front of the pursuing hounds, heading toward a barred gate. "There he is!"

"Out of the way, you," shouted the huntsmen, who had galloped up behind them and overheard Morgan. "This one's ours!"

And as the riders charged through the children, knocking them aside, Sid turned, saw the dogs, and clambered desperately over the gate.

"Gee whiz!" said Avril angrily, picking herself up as the policemen, Mr. Coatsworth, Miss Beaver, and the farmer and his wife caught up with them. "That bunch doesn't have any manners!" she fumed. The rest of the children jumped up too, and with a fresh burst of energy ran toward the gate, just as the huntsmen disappeared over it.

"Goodness!" said Miss Beaver as they all peered over the gate, for Sid had stopped suddenly in his tracks, turned, and with a cry of terror zigzagged his way back past the men on horseback, with the dogs snapping at his heels.

"Oh! Look!" cried Avril in delight, seeing what

had made Sid change direction. She opened the gate for him to stagger through. "A *bull!*"

And as the rest of the class, the dogs, the policemen, Mr. Coatsworth, Miss Beaver, and the farmer and his wife leaped on Sid, the huntsmen wheeled their horses around in alarm. The bull, pounding the earth with its hooves and snorting, was thundering toward them.

The riders shrieked in horror, then, clinging tightly to the necks of the frightened horses, they galloped toward the gate that Avril (transfixed with joy at the sight of a bull) was still holding open. Jostling each other to get out of the way, they fought furiously to get through it as the angry bull pounded up behind them.

While the children watched in amazement, the bull charged first one, then another rider, scattering them in different directions until they had vanished completely.

"Oh!" Avril sighed. "Isn't he *wonderful?*"

"You naughty boy, Buttons," said Mrs. Rams-

bottom, letting go of Sid's nose as the bull snorted in satisfaction, then trotted meekly across to her.

"I can't think what came over him," she added, stroking the beast's head and leading him back into the field.

"He's usually as gentle as a lamb," she explained to the nervous children, closing the gate again. "It must have been the red coats that upset him."

In all the commotion, the dogs had managed to squeeze their way past the children to get at Sid's pockets. And having eaten all the licorice balls, they wandered aimlessly across the fields.

"Well," said Sergeant Pattison after he'd snapped a pair of handcuffs onto Sid's wrists and picked up the two satchels, "I can't thank you children enough." He beamed as he patted the two bags. "There'll be a reward of course, and I wouldn't be surprised if you weren't all National Heroes by tomorrow morning!"

"Well!" Miss Beaver said. "If you don't mind, I think our National Heroes ought to have their lunch now."

The children, Miss Beaver, and the farmer's wife took a shortcut across the fields to the farm. Sergeant Pattison and his men took Sid to the police station, while Mr. Ramsbottom went to collect the tractor and trailer, and Mr. Coatsworth went back to the bus, put Mr. and Mrs. Ramsbottom's tandem bicycle in it, and drove around to the farm to meet them.

12 "What a Scoop!"

When Mrs. Ramsbottom saw the dried-up sandwiches (which the birds had gotten at anyway), she insisted on bringing out a huge ham, cold chicken, a dish of tomatoes, freshly baked bread, and an enormous slab of farmhouse butter.

"Well!" said Miss Beaver after they'd finished the delicious apple pie and jug of thick cream that Mrs. Ramsbottom had brought out for dessert. "What an exciting day it turned out to be, just think . . ."

"Excuse me," a voice interrupted eagerly.

"Goodness!" said Miss Beaver in surprise as a man's head popped up from behind a hedge.

"You wouldn't mind if I interviewed you, would you?" the young man inquired anxiously, his eyes darting from one child to another.

"Oh, marvelous, marvelous!" he exclaimed, when Miss Beaver shook her head.

"I'm Old Amos from the *Clarion*," he added, leaping agilely over the hedge and nearly tripping over Avril's coat in his haste to get to them.

"Old Amos and His Country Rambles," he explained, looking at Miss Beaver's puzzled face. "Every Thursday. Approximately two hundred words. Although to be honest," he added, straightening his tie and flicking a piece of mud off his highly polished shoe with his handkerchief, "it's not really my line at all. In fact," he muttered, wrinkling his nose and looking distastefully across the fields, "I don't even like the country."

"Old Amos," Mr. Coatsworth repeated thoughtfully. "Ah!" he said, slapping his leg. "I remember

now. I read one of your articles once about sheep clipping.''

"Oh!" said Miss Beaver as the dapper young man grimaced at the mention of sheep. "You're a reporter!"

"A reporter!" echoed the children excitedly. "A reporter. He's come for our story!"

"Actually," the young man said, frowning, "I was supposed to be covering the local Hunt, but I can't seem to find it, so I thought I might pepper up the article with an interview with children." He glanced at Miss Beaver. "You are from a school, I expect? London?" he inquired eagerly. Miss Beaver nodded again. "Good," continued the reporter. "Well, if you could perhaps give me your views . . ."

"It was like this," Avril interrupted. "Miss Beaver left her bag on the bus! . . ."

"Then it got mixed up with the robbers," Morgan added.

"And when they realized, they dressed up as Mr. and Mrs. Ramsbottom . . ." said Dominic.

"And locked the real farmer and his wife in the bedroom," said Akbar.

"And don't forget the chase," Jessica chimed in, "where we nearly crashed lots of times and they'd got teacher on the bus and were threatening her with a gun, and . . ."

"But it was the licorice balls that did it really," Avril interrupted as the reporter looked at them blankly, laughed uncertainly, then turned to Miss Beaver.

"Marvelous imagination, children," he murmured, "marvelous!"

"But it's absolutely true!" Miss Beaver said in surprise. "Didn't you know? The children captured the robbers, and in fact," she added proudly, "Sergeant Pattison said they would probably be National Heroes by tomorrow!"

"And we're getting a reward too," Avril finished grandly.

The young man sank to the ground, staring at Miss Beaver in disbelief. "You mean to say," he asked weakly, "that they actually caught two criminals?"

"Yes," said Miss Beaver firmly.

"And retrieved the money that the robbers had stolen," Mr. Coatsworth added.

"Oh my!" said the reporter dreamily. "What a story! What a *story*!!" he repeated, striking his head with his fist and jumping up. "Children," he shouted excitedly, "allow me to introduce myself, Mike Spilligan, special crime reporter! Now, where's my pen?" he muttered, searching feverishly in his pockets. "Oh, imagine it, imagine it," he murmured to himself. "What a scoop. No more nasty sheep, no more foot-and-mouth, no more foot rot,

NO MORE OLD AMOS!'' he shouted triumphantly, pulling a pen and a notebook from his inside pocket and flourishing them at the bewildered
children. And after he'd taken all the details down,
he ran to the farmhouse and telephoned his story to
every major newspaper and TV network. When all
the children had had a last look at the bull, said
good-bye to Mr. and Mrs. Ramsbottom, and climbed
onto the bus to go home, he was still dancing around
the farmyard ecstatically, murmuring, ''What a
scoop, what a scoop!''

13 Welcome Home, Heroes

"Well!" Miss Beaver smiled at the children, who were going through the events of the day, detail by detail. "We're nearly home now."

"And I must say," proclaimed Mr. Coatsworth, "it's the best school outing I've ever been on!"

"And me!" said Morgan, Dominic, Jessica, Akbar, and all the rest of the third grade, thinking about the exciting chase across the fields and the capture of Sid and Bert.

"And they did have a bull after all," Avril added, sighing contentedly.

"Goodness," exclaimed Miss Beaver as the bus turned into New End, "what a lot of noise!"

The children pressed their noses to the bus windows to see what was happening.

"Wow!" shouted Morgan, looking at the crowd of people outside the school who surged forward, cheering and waving, when they saw the bus approaching.

"Look!" cried Dominic. "Television cameras!"

"And reporters!" shouted Akbar. Photographers jostled each other, taking pictures of the bus.

"Hello, Dad!" Avril screamed, opening the bus window and waving to a figure at the back of the crowd. "I saw a bull!"

"Oooh!" whispered Jessica as Mr. Coatsworth

stopped the bus to avoid running over the reporters. "I hope we don't get trampled to death like that cowboy did in the film."

Miss Beaver had difficulty in opening the doors because of the crowd, and it wasn't until the policemen linked arms and formed a clearing around the bus that she, Mr. Coatsworth, and the children could step down.

The crowd went wild with excitement. The waiting parents were so overcome they had to blow their noses, and the children from the other classes, who had wriggled their way to the front of the crowd to get a better view, started chanting

> "2—4—6—8
> Who do we appreciate?
> The third grade!"

The headmaster, who'd wriggled to the front of the crowd too, clapped his hands together in delight and beamed with pride.

"Goodness," Miss Beaver murmured as the mayor

stepped forward to greet them, "that young man from the *Clarion* certainly spread the news!"

"Welcome home, heroes," said the mayor, holding his hand up for silence. "I would like to take this opportunity to invite you all to a civic reception in your honor, where the Chief Constable of Scotland Yard will present you with the reward."

"Hooray!" screamed the crowd, stamping their feet in approval.

"And now," he added, smiling at Miss Beaver, "perhaps you could tell us personally how you first became involved with the bank robbers."

"Well," said Miss Beaver shyly, "it all started when I mislaid my satchel . . ."

"Let's see it, Miss!" chorused the reporters, who had their cameras poised to take a picture of it.

"Certainly." Miss Beaver smiled.

And while she climbed into the bus to look for it, the headmaster, who had ducked under the policemen's legs, waved his arms wildly in the air.

"Three cheers for Morgan!" he shouted.

"HIP HIP HOORAY!" the crowd screamed.

"Three cheers for Dominic!"

"HIP HIP HOORAY!"

"Three cheers for Jessica!"

"HIP HIP HOORAY!"

"Three cheers for Akbar!"

"HIP HIP HOORAY!"

"Three cheers for Avril!"

"HIP HIP HOORAY!!!"

When the headmaster had been through the children of the third grade name by name, and Miss Beaver and Mr. Coatsworth too, and the crowd had roared themselves hoarse, Miss Beaver reappeared.

"Oh dear!" she said to the expectant crowd, laughing awkwardly, "I'm dreadfully sorry. But— er," she paused guiltily, "I seem to have mislaid it!"

Pat Hutchins's career in children's books began with the publication of *Rosie's Walk*, a 1968 ALA Notable Book. Since then she has written and illustrated many highly acclaimed picture books, including *The Wind Blew*, the 1974 winner of England's prestigious Kate Greenaway Medal, and short novels for older readers.

Ms. Hutchins was born in Yorkshire, England, and grew up in the surrounding countryside. Pursuing her childhood desire to be an artist, she attended Leeds College of Art, where she specialized in illustration. She now lives in London with her husband, Laurence, who also happens to be the illustrator of this book. They have two sons.